2 7th

The Accidental Twins

The
Accidental Twins

❧

ANGELA BULL

illustrated by Jill Bennett

FABER AND FABER
London and Boston

First published in 1982
by Faber and Faber Limited
3 Queen Square London WC1N 3AU
Printed in Great Britain by
Redwood Burn Ltd., Trowbridge
All rights reserved

British Library Cataloguing in Publication Data

Bull, Angela
The accidental twins
I. Title
823′.914[J]   PZ7

ISBN 0–571–11761–9

Chapter One

THEY WERE accidental twins, not real twins, because they weren't sisters. Their names were Susan Green and Sally Gray. They both had blue eyes and short brown hair, and of course they were exactly the same age. They had discovered this on the day they met—their very first day at school.

"Can anyone tell me when their birthday is?" the teacher had asked her class of new five-year-olds, and Susan, who had been told what to do at school, shot her hand up.

"Mine's on May the first," she announced.

"What a lovely day for a birthday," said the teacher. "May Day."

Sally Gray opened her eyes very wide. "I think my birthday's on May Day too," she said. "It might be."

"Aren't you sure?" asked Susan scornfully.

Sally shook her head.

The teacher ran her finger down the class register. "Sally Gray—May first; Susan Green—May first. You two must be twins; accidental twins. How nice!"

The other children gazed with interest at Susan and Sally.

"They look alike," said someone.

"Same socks," another child pointed out.

"Everyone has white socks," said Susan.

"They even have the same initials," said the teacher. "Stand up, both of you. Let's see if you're the same height."

They were, exactly.

"How lovely," said the teacher, "to have twins in the class; accidental twins!"

But strangely enough neither Susan nor Sally thought it was lovely. People like to be themselves, and just themselves; not a copy of somebody else. Susan and Sally both felt upset, and even a bit cross, that they should be in the same class as a person who looked like them, and had the same socks, the same initials, and the same birthday. It wouldn't be so bad if she was nice, they both thought; but Sally had already decided that Susan, with her scornful manner, was going to be superior and conceited, while Susan had decided that Sally, who wasn't certain when her birthday was, must be a silly little thing.

So matters started off on the wrong foot for the accidental twins.

As they moved up the school they were always put into the same class. The teachers imagined that, because they were twins, they would be great friends, but they weren't. Susan was clever. She

worked hard, and got ahead of everyone in reading and maths. Sally wasn't so good at lessons, but she shone in the playground. She ran faster, jumped farther, and managed balls better than any other girl of her age. Some people admired Susan, and some people admired Sally; but they didn't admire each other.

Susan lived with her mother and grandmother. They did grown-up things, like going to concerts, and watching serious television programmes. Sally lived with her parents and three brothers, and they did carefree, harum-scarum things, like hiking all week-end with sleeping bags in their rucksacks, and sleeping under the stars.

Susan's neat white house was perched on a hill-side, with fifteen steps between the pavement and the front door; and that—said unkind people—was why Susan was so stuck up. Sally's old house was set in a garden full of trees for the children to climb; and that—said unkind people—was why Sally was such a monkey. But some children loved to be invited to Susan's home, where they played board games, with all the proper rules, on a proper card table; and other children loved the wild times they had at Sally's, with picnics in the tree house, and chasings among the bushes. Only somehow Susan never went to Sally's house, and Sally never went to Susan's.

All the way up the school they seemed to be in competition. There was, for example, the time of the great skipping craze. Susan's mother bought her an expensive skipping-rope from a country craft shop. It had bobbin handles, and a light, swishing rope. All through Sunday Susan practised on the path behind her house, until she could skip perfectly, backwards and forwards. She enjoyed the skipping, but she also cherished a secret hope that she might be able to skip better than Sally. The hope grew stronger when she arrived at school on Monday morning and saw a grubby length of plastic rope, hacked from a clothes-line, trailing untidily from Sally's anorak pocket. Susan stroked the bobbin handles of her own rope. She thought that Sally was in for a surprise.

When the mid-morning bell clanged, everyone rushed into the playground. Susan chose a wide, empty space where she could be seen, and began to skip, swinging her rope in a steady rhythm, over and under. But no one was watching. They were all staring in another direction. There were shouts of— "Look at Sally!" For with her clumsy rope whipping like the wind, Sally was skipping an endless series of "double-throughs", bounding like a ball, hardly touching the ground, and no one had any attention to spare for Susan's careful skipping and expensive rope.

Sometimes things were the other way round, and it was Susan's turn to excel. There was the time when they were asked to write and illustrate an account of

some bird they had studied on their own. The best piece of work, the teacher said, would be pinned up in the hall.

For once Sally felt she could do herself credit. There was a rookery near her garden, and she had been watching the big, sooty rooks, flapping round their ink-blot nests. She tried her hardest to write neatly, and draw accurately, so that her account would be the best. Pencilling in the glossy black feathers, she glanced at the children nearby. They all seemed to have chosen robins. There were enough red breasts to suggest an epidemic of bird measles. Across the room she saw Susan picking up a red felt-tip, and she sighed with satisfaction. Her rook would really stand out among that crowd of robins!

When the papers had been handed in they were supposed to get on with their maths, but Sally was too excited to bother. She watched the teacher looking at each sheet, and crossed her fingers.

At last the moment came. Sally held her breath.

"They were all very good," said the teacher, "but this one was outstanding." She held up a sheet of paper, topped by a brilliantly coloured parrot, its plumage a riot of scarlet and yellow and blue. "What a lot you know about parrots, Susan."

"We went to a Bird Garden on Saturday," said Susan calmly. She had known her work would be the best. It always was.

Sally could have cried with disappointment.

And then came the spring with the two big muddles between the accidental twins.

Chapter Two

NOT FAR from the school there was a busy main road. Cars, buses and lorries thundered up and down all day long, so there was a lollipop lady called Mrs Jones to help the children to cross. She had done the job for years, and knew all the children nearly as well as they knew her.

Towards the end of the spring term, when Susan and Sally were eight, the head teacher told the children that Mrs Jones was going to retire. She was getting too old to stand outside on cold, wet days, holding up the traffic. As a way of saying thank you and good-bye, the children were asked to bring some money towards a present for Mrs Jones.

"What do you think we'll give her?" wondered Susan, trying to imagine what she would want if she were an old lady. "I guess she'd like a big handbag, with lots of pockets."

"I'd want a new colour television, a really enormous one," said Jane, who was a friend of Sally's.

"My Gran got a coffee set when she retired from work," said Susan's special friend, Paula.

"What do you think she'd like, Sally?" asked Jane.

Sally had no idea what a person of sixty might want. She could only think of what she would like herself. "A puppy," she suggested.

The scorn on Susan's face told her at once that she had said something silly. "Seeing Mrs Jones is retiring because she doesn't like going out when it's cold and wet," said Susan, "she certainly won't want a puppy to exercise. Puppies have to be taken for lots of walks."

When Susan spoke like that it was no use arguing. Sally turned away, feeling snubbed, and pretended to be busy at her desk.

But all the guesses, from handbags to puppies, were wrong. Mrs Jones asked to be given an electric mixer, and because, when it had been bought, there was still some money over, the teachers decided she should have a bouquet of flowers as well. The mixer and the bouquet would be presented on the last day of term, at Assembly, and parents were invited to come too, and say goodbye to Mrs Jones.

On the day before the last day of term, the teacher in Susan's and Sally's class was clearing out her desk. Susan wished she could help. The piles of papers coming out of the drawers looked much more interesting than the rather dull book she was reading. As she gazed across the room, she caught the teacher's eye.

"Oh, Susan," said the teacher, "this folder has to go to the Head's office. Will you take it for me, please."

Susan jumped up eagerly. She loved doing errands. Sally, her head bent over her book, sighed with thankfulness that she had not been sent. She hated being given responsible jobs. She was always sure she would make a mess of them.

In the office the head teacher, Miss Macdonald, was telephoning. Susan laid the folder on her desk, and was tiptoeing away, when Miss Macdonald covered the receiver with her hand. "Wait a minute, Susan," she whispered, and spoke into the telephone again.

There must be another errand, thought Susan. She stood in the middle of the office, feeling import-

ant. The office was an interesting place too. She liked the Head's big desk, and the other desk where the new secretary usually sat, and she liked the shelves of books, and the timetables and charts on the walls.

Presently Miss Macdonald put down the telephone. She smiled at Susan. "I'm glad you came in," she said, "because there's something I want to ask you to do."

"Yes?" said Susan.

"We need somebody who's sensible and careful to present the bouquet to Mrs Jones tomorrow. I thought you might be the best person to do it."

Susan went pink with delight. "I'd be very careful," she promised.

"Good," said Miss Macdonald. "Don't tell anyone, because we don't want Mrs Jones to hear even a whisper about the flowers. They're to be a surprise. Come to my office tomorrow morning, before Assembly, and the secretary will give you the flowers."

"Yes, Miss Macdonald," said Susan. She walked sedately out of the room, but inside she was bubbling with excitement. She, Susan Green, had been chosen out of the whole school. It was a pity she couldn't tell her friends, but Miss Macdonald should see that she could keep a secret.

As she left, the new secretary came into the office.

"Did you notice that child?" Miss Macdonald inquired. "I've asked her to present the bouquet to Mrs Jones tomorrow, so will you see that she gets it?"

"Certainly," agreed the secretary. She wasn't very familiar with the children yet, but she thought she could remember the girl Miss Macdonald meant: the one with short brown hair and blue eyes, who was about eight.

Chapter Three

SALLY SET off early for school on the last morning of term. Her mother was coming to Assembly, but Sally didn't wait for her, or for her brothers. By arriving early, she could have extra time with her friends.

Handstands were the latest craze, and in the playground a line of waving legs were already kicking against the school wall. Sally was extremely good at handstands. Dropping the carrier bag she had brought to take her things home in, she rushed to join her friends.

When the big bell clanged for Assembly, Sally lingered outside. It was more fun doing handstands than sitting in a tidy row on the floor of the hall. But she didn't want a scolding for being late, so at the last moment she dashed in, tossed off her coat in the cloakroom—and remembered her carrier bag.

"I've left my bag in the playground," she told Jane.

"Get it, then," Jane advised. "There's still time."

Near the front door was the Head's office, and as Sally whisked past, the secretary, who was hovering

anxiously, seized her arm.

"There you are at last!" she exclaimed. "I've been waiting. It's in here." And she pulled Sally into the office.

"What do you mean?" asked Sally in surprise.

"The bouquet for Mrs Jones. This."

A huge bunch of yellow and white spring flowers, wrapped in cellophane and tied with gold ribbon, lay on a table. The secretary held it out towards Sally, who backed nervously away.

"I don't want it," she protested.

"Nonsense. You're to present it to Mrs Jones."

"Me?"

"Of course. Didn't Miss Macdonald tell you? She chose you yesterday. Just smooth your hair down, dear. It's a pity no one suggested you put on a clean frock."

"Nobody told me anything. And I can't—I don't want to—" stammered poor Sally.

"It's perfectly simple. You take the bouquet up to the front after Miss Macdonald's speech, and give it to Mrs Jones. Just say—'Thank you, Mrs Jones, and we wish you a happy retirement'. Mrs Jones is in the hall now, with Miss Macdonald, and we don't want her to see you with the flowers, so we'll creep in at the side, and sit behind the piano."

Sally had never felt so frightened in her life. It was like a nightmare from which it was impossible to escape. The secretary hustled her through a side

door to a corner of the hall where they were partly concealed by the piano—partly, but not completely. Certainly Mrs Jones and Miss Macdonald were invisible, but Sally could see several rows of children, with some mothers behind them, and even a few fathers and grandmothers. They would all see her presenting the flowers to Mrs Jones! Sally felt hot and cold all over. She stared down at the bouquet, and saw instead the dirtiness of her hands, after all those handstands, and the splash on her dress where she had spilled ice cream yesterday.

"Hurry up, Mum," begged Susan.
They had been late leaving the house because Mrs

Green had had to ring the place where she worked, and explain that she was going to school to see her daughter present a bouquet. The telephoning took ages, and Susan, prancing about in her best pink skirt and white jersey, thought her mother would never finish talking. As they approached the school, she could see that the playground was empty.

"They must be in Assembly already, Mum," she said. "You go straight to the hall. I've got to collect the flowers."

She tapped importantly at the office door. There was no reply. After a pause she tapped again. Still no one came. At last, very daringly, Susan opened the door. There was nobody in the room; no secretary, and no flowers.

At that moment another teacher appeared from the staffroom next door.

"What are you doing, Susan?" she asked. "You should be in the hall."

"No, I shouldn't," Susan replied. "I haven't got the flowers for Mrs Jones yet."

"Are you presenting them? I see."

The teacher went into the office and looked around. "How funny! That new secretary must have moved them," she said. "She's probably in the hall. You'd better run and ask her."

It was easier said than done. As Susan opened the hall door, everybody stood up for the first hymn. In a hall crowded with children and parents, it was impossible to start hunting for the secretary. Angry and puzzled, Susan slipped into her usual place. What *was* she supposed to do? How could she present the flowers if no one gave them to her? She had been longing for the moment when she walked gracefully forward, with everyone watching, and handed the bouquet to Mrs Jones. She had dressed in her best clothes specially. And now, unless someone acted quickly, she might miss the opportunity. She stared desperately round, but Sally and the secretary were out of sight.

Behind the piano, Sally felt worse and worse. Why had she been chosen, she wondered frantically. She would be sure to fall over her own feet, and drop the bouquet. Why hadn't they chosen someone like Susan, who would do it well? She heard Miss Macdonald beginning to talk about Mrs Jones, but she couldn't listen. She gazed at her black fingers, and felt her heart thud agonizingly inside her stained frock.

"Now!" hissed the secretary suddenly, prodding Sally to her feet.

Sally emerged trembling from behind the piano, and picked her way between the rows of children, scarlet in the face, and clutching the flowers upside-down. Mrs Jones seemed a mile away, standing there in her lollipop lady's white coat and cap.

"Sally!" exclaimed Miss Macdonald, sounding surprised and annoyed.

25

It was the last straw. Everything seemed to go clean out of Sally's head. She knew there were words to say, and a name to remember, but she had forgotten them all.

"Here—" she gasped—"Here are some flowers, Mrs—er—Mrs Lollipop!"

Such a peal of laughter broke out that Sally could have fallen through the floor with shame, but Mrs Jones stepped towards her, smiling, and took the bouquet.

"Thank you, love. It's beautiful!" she said, and she turned back to the other children. "It's all very well laughing at Sally's little mistake," she told them, "but I think Mrs Lollipop is a very good name for me, and there's nobody I'd like better to give me a bouquet than Sally Gray."

Suddenly everyone clapped, Miss Macdonald nodded, and the ordeal was over. Weak with relief, Sally stumbled back to her own class. From a row behind she saw Susan, glaring furiously at her.

"You must have known something was wrong when they gave you the flowers," snapped Susan, as they left the hall.

"I didn't," protested Sally.

"How could anyone choose you? Your frock's a mess, and your hands are filthy."

"I didn't want to be chosen."

"And then to forget her name—"

26

"I didn't mean to."

"Mrs Jones was pleased," Jane pointed out.

"She only said that to be kind. Things would have been much better if I'd presented the flowers. And I should have done! It was all a stupid mistake." Susan turned away, nearly crying with anger and disappointment.

"Well, you shouldn't look so alike," said Jane. "It only happened because you're accidental twins."

Chapter Four

FORTUNATELY THE Easter holidays started the next day, allowing everyone's feelings to cool down. Susan was soothed by some pleasant outings, while Sally would have forgotten the whole affair if the daffodils, dancing gaily in her garden, hadn't occasionally reminded her of that disastrous bouquet of spring flowers.

When school began again, the May Day birthdays seemed very close.

"You'll be nine a week on Thursday," said Mrs Green to Susan, as they ate their tea on the first day of term. "I suppose you'll want a birthday party."

Susan frowned, considering. Every year she had invited a few girls from school—but of course never Sally—to tea on her birthday. They had played Passing the Parcel and Musical Statues, with chocolates and pencils for prizes. Mrs Green had made a delicious tea, and the guests had gone home with slices of cake, and presents prettily wrapped in coloured paper.

Thinking about it, Susan suddenly felt bored. She was tired of parties. She wanted to do something different.

"Could we go out somewhere? Not the Bird Garden, but perhaps the pictures?"

Mrs Green fetched the local paper, and scanned its columns.

"How lucky!" she exclaimed. "A ballet company's coming to the King's Theatre for the week of your birthday. Would you like to go to that?"

Again Susan considered. She remembered ballet programmes on television. Orchestras played, and dancers in dresses like soft white snowflakes glided and pirouetted and spun.

"I'd like to go," she began, "and could I take Paula and Debbie and—"

"Wait a minute," her mother interrupted. "The tickets are terribly expensive. If you and I and Granny go, I shall only be able to afford one more ticket. Can you choose just one friend?"

"Only one?" protested Susan.

"Yes—unless you'd rather have an ordinary party instead."

"I want to go to the ballet," said Susan firmly, "but I'm not quite sure who to choose."

"I met Mrs Gray this morning," said Susan's mother. "She mentioned that Sally was very keen on dancing. Would you like to ask her? It would show that you had forgiven her for that mistake over the bouquet, and Mrs Gray said she was really most upset about it. Why not have her? It would be a birthday treat for her as well."

"No, thank you," Susan replied swiftly, "not Sally." More than ever she hated to be reminded that they were twins. "Shall we ask Karen?"

Karen was Susan's cousin, and nearly twelve.

"Good idea," said Mrs Green. "I'll ring about the tickets now. We'd better go to the Saturday afternoon performance. If we go on Thursday evening, you'll be tired for school on Friday."

Susan gave a wail of dismay. "I want to go on my birthday."

"Don't be silly. It'll be just as nice on Saturday."

Sally, her parents, and her three brothers, Tony, Peter and Jeremy, were sitting round the kitchen table, eating stew, and discussing Sally's birthday.

"Why don't you have a picnic, Sally?" suggested Tony.

"We could go swimming first," said Peter.

"Or to the Sports Centre," said Jeremy.

"I can't fit many extra people into the car," said Mr Gray.

"Well, stay at home then," said Tony, "and play rounders in the garden."

"Bulldog's Charge," said Peter.

"Hide and seek," said Jeremy.

"If it's fine we could get out the barbecue things," said Mrs Gray. "Sally's birthday could be our first barbecue of the year."

"We could have chicken legs," cried Tony.

"Hot dogs," shouted Peter.

"Hamburgers," pleaded Jeremy.

"They seem to be settling it for you, Sally," said Mrs Gray. "Would you be happy with a barbecue?"

"Oh, yes," said Sally. She was used to having things settled for her.

"Ask plenty of people," said Tony. "Then we can have two proper rounders teams."

"I wonder if you should invite Susan Green," said Mrs Gray. "I met her mother in town this morning, and I got the impression that Susan must lead a rather dull life. She's an only child, and she always seems to be with grown-ups. It might make a nice change for her to come to your barbecue, and it would show there were no hard feelings over that business of the bouquet."

Sally thought for a moment. She didn't really dislike Susan; in fact she quite agreed that it would have been much better if Susan had presented the flowers. But Susan irritated her by always behaving as if she were more important than Sally, as if it were somehow Sally's fault that she also had her birthday on May the first; and she could be so snubbing.

"I don't think Susan would want to come," said Sally. "She'll be having her own party. I'll choose some other people."

Chapter Five

THE SUBJECT of the birthdays came up in conversation at school next day, when Jane bounced into the cloakroom as Sally and Susan were taking off their coats.

"Hello, twins!" she greeted them. "It'll soon be your birthday, won't it?"

At the word "twins", Susan stiffened, and Sally felt uneasy. Neither spoke, but Jane didn't notice.

"Are you having parties?" she demanded.

Susan was ready to answer this. "I'm not having an ordinary party," she said. "I'm going to the ballet with my cousin Karen, who's nearly twelve."

From behind the coat-pegs, Sally gazed at Susan, her eyes wide with longing. More than anything in the world, she wanted to go to a ballet.

"Where is it on?" she asked.

"Here, in town; at the King's Theatre."

If only, Sally yearned—but her birthday treat had been arranged, and Jane was asking about it. Sally tried to sound bright.

"I'm having a barbecue in the garden," she said. "We'll grill sausages and chicken legs, and play rounders and hide and seek."

"Good!" said Jane. "We always have fun in your garden. Have you ever played there, Susan?"

"No," Susan replied, shrugging her shoulders as if she couldn't care less.

"It's gorgeous," said Jane; "so many trees to climb—"

But Susan had walked out of the cloakroom.

As soon as the bell clanged for the end of afternoon lessons, Sally snatched her coat and flew. Her house wasn't far away, and before Susan had even left the school playground, Sally had raced into the garden, and over to her mother, who was planting out peas.

"Mum, could I go to the ballet? Susan's going for her birthday treat."

Mrs Gray looked up in surprise. "Is there a ballet on? I didn't know."

"It's going to be at the theatre next week. Oh, Mum, I'd love to go for my birthday. Do let's. Please!"

"I thought you wanted a barbecue," said Mrs Gray, rather bewildered by Sally's unexpected request.

"I can have a barbecue any time. I'd prefer the ballet."

She gazed pleadingly at her mother, and Mrs Gray stood up. "I'll wash this mud off, and then I'll ring the theatre, and see if I can get some tickets."

"Thank you!"

Bursting with relief and excitement, Sally flung herself on to the old car tyre which dangled by a rope from the branch of a tree. She was swinging wildly, feet flying, as Susan walked slowly up the road.

The Greens had very little garden. The fifteen steps between the pavement and the front door simply climbed past a garage, dug out from the hillside. At the back of the house was the paved path where Susan had practised skipping, and above it the ground rose steeply again in a rockery covered with creeping plants. Susan found this very unsatisfactory. She longed for space to play, for shady trees to lie under, and beds full of bright flowers. Now, remembering Jane's words, she paused to look over Sally's gate.

The garden was full of colour. Candy-pink cherry petals fluttered down on to drifts of scarlet and white tulips. Trees, misty with spring green, spread higgledy-piggledy across a wide stretch of grass, with sweeping branches that seemed to invite the most timid person to climb.

Susan stared longingly. If only she could run through those green spaces, or bury her nose in the flowers—

Sally's flying heels suddenly caught her eye. She hurried on up the road. It was no good wishing she could go to Sally's barbecue. Her treat was to be the ballet.

35

Mrs Gray came out of the house.

"I'm very sorry, Sally," she called, "but there aren't any tickets left for the ballet. Every performance is sold out."

Sally tumbled off the tyre, her face stricken.

"Oh, Mum! I *did* want to go."

"I'm sorry," said Mrs Gray again. "I'm afraid it's too late."

Chapter Six

"I WISH WE had a garden," sighed Susan at tea-time.

"Do you?" her mother asked, surprised. "Why?"

"I'd like to lie in long grass, and watch the flowers growing!"

"You'd have to watch for a long time," replied Mrs Green laughing. "But it's no good wishing for a garden. I wouldn't have time to look after it, and Granny's too stiff."

"I could look after it," said Susan.

"You don't realize what hard work it would be. We're very well off with just our path and rockery."

Mrs Green nodded with such finality that Susan knew the subject was closed. She drooped sadly over her plate.

"As tomorrow's Saturday," her mother went on, "shall we go shopping? I want to buy you some new clothes for the ballet."

Susan brightened up at once. She loved new clothes. "What can I get?" she asked.

"I saw a very pretty blue velvet pinafore teamed with a blue and white blouse in Willis's shop window," said Mrs Green. "We might go and look at that."

Susan smiled, forgetting her lack of garden. Velvet was her favourite material, and she always looked nice in blue.

Sally, meanwhile, was trying to forget her disappointment, but she wasn't very successful. Everyone in her family felt sorry about it, but ballet tickets can't be produced out of thin air. When Mrs Gray went upstairs to kiss Sally good night, she plumped herself down on the bed, and put her arm round her sad little daughter.

"Poor Sally," she said. "It's a shame about the ballet, but you'll like the barbecue, won't you?"

"I suppose so," was all Sally could answer.

"I'm afraid the boys stampeded you into choosing a barbecue," said Mrs Gray. "They do tend to sweep you along if you let them. Perhaps we should stop expecting you to want the same things as they do. I wonder if the time is coming when you'll have to strike out on your own and be different."

"It might be," said Sally.

"Well, make do with the barbecue this year, but next year we won't let the boys decide for you. And I've been thinking about your birthday present. I know we considered roller skates, but would you like something a bit more feminine? How about a pretty dress, to wear if we ever went to the ballet?"

"A dress?" Sally was startled. Her drawers and cupboards were full of jeans and tee-shirts, with some plain skirts for school. She'd never even wished for a pretty dress.

"It would make a change," urged her mother.

"What would the boys say?"

"Forget the boys for once. You'll wear the dress, not them."

Sally giggled. "It might be rather nice," she said, trying vainly to picture herself in—what? Lace ruffles? A skirt like a tutu?

"We'll go shopping in the morning."

"Sally in frills! We can't wait," teased the boys at breakfast next morning.

Sally began to feel alarmed. "Don't buy me anything fancy, Mum," she begged. "I'm really a jeans and tee-shirt person."

"If you boys don't shut up," said Mrs Gray, "I'll buy you pink silk shirts and make you all wear them! As for you, Sally, there was a blue velvet pinafore in Willis's window yesterday, with a nice blue and white blouse. They'd suit you very well, and they weren't a bit frilly."

Sally's fears melted away when she tried on the outfit her mother had seen. Lace edged the collar and cuffs of the blouse, and the pinafore was cut into a full, bell-like skirt; but even the most critical brother couldn't call the clothes fancy.

"Prettiness without fussiness," remarked the shop assistant. "Just what most people want. We've another of these outfits in stock, but it's sure to sell quickly."

"I don't think the boys will scoff," said Sally, as they left the shop.

"Scoff!" echoed Mrs Gray. "Certainly not! Look, is that Susan Green crossing the road with her mother?"

"Yes. I'm glad they haven't seen us," said Sally. "Can I wear my new clothes on my birthday?"

Chapter Seven

At last the birthday came. Sally was woken at half past six by a horde of shouting brothers.

"Wake up, Sally! Many happy returns of the day!"

Tony tugged back the curtains, and sunlight poured into the room. "Smashing day, perfect for a barbecue," he said.

"Good." Sally sat up, rubbing her eyes.

The boys tossed little parcels of sweets on to the bed. Sally opened them, and shared the sweets round.

"We've got you a rounders bat. It's on the breakfast table," said Jeremy.

"Shut up! It was meant to be a surprise."

Tony and Peter leaped on Jeremy and pummelled him. He hit back, and the house resounded with shrieks and crashes, as Sally threw her pillow into the fray.

Things were very different at the Greens'. Susan woke at her usual time, and lay peacefully for a few minutes, watching the pattern of sunlight on her curtains. Then she remembered her new clothes, and how her mother her said she could wear them that day if she was careful to keep them clean. With a bound, she was out of bed, and opening the wardrobe, where the new pinafore and blouse were hanging. She took them gently down, smoothing the lace-edged collar, and stroking the velvet. They were a birthday treat in themselves. No one else at school would have such lovely clothes.

As soon as she had dressed, she ran downstairs to find a stack of cards and ribbon-tied parcels by her plate. There was a writing case from her mother, and a pictorial encyclopedia from her grandmother.

"It's the fattest encyclopedia I've seen," she

exclaimed in delight. "650 pages—I'm sure that's more than the big one in our class at school."

Everything was perfect until she opened the card from Karen, and then she had a disappointment.

"I'm sorry I shan't be able to come to the ballet on Saturday," wrote Karen, "but I'm playing in a netball match."

"Oh dear!" wailed Susan. "Karen can't come to the ballet."

Mrs Green read the message. "We'll have to find another person to join us," she said. "I wonder if Aunty Enid would come."

"Not Aunty Enid!" protested Susan. She wasn't very fond of her aunt who chattered ceaselessly to the grown-ups, but never to Susan.

"Don't be silly," said her mother. "Aunty Enid loves the ballet. I'll give her a ring tonight."

For a moment Susan felt inclined to sulk, but the sight of her presents was very cheering. She began to make a pile of the ones she wanted to show her friends at school.

"Don't forget the card for Sally," prompted her grandmother.

Mrs Green had bought the card. It had a picture of a little girl with long yellow hair feeding a kitten, and privately Susan thought it most unsuitable for Sally, but she had dutifully written "from Susan" inside. She put it ready with her writing case, her encyclo-pedia, and some other books.

43

She felt very laden as she set off along the road: important too, to be carrying so many things, only it slowed her down. The children whom she usually walked with had all got ahead. When she reached Sally's house, she couldn't help stopping to peep over the gate at those green expanses, dappled with sunlight, which stretched so enticingly away.

"Hi!" a voice shouted, and Jane ran up. "Happy birthday!"

"Thank you," said Susan.

"Aren't you longing for this afternoon?" Jane went on. "Sally's barbecue, I mean."

"I shan't be there," said Susan.

"Of course; you're going to the ballet."

"No, that's not till Saturday."

"Oh!" said Jane surprised. She hunted in her duffle bag. "I've got a card for you. Here—no, that's Sally's. This is yours. Open it. Look, there's one you haven't opened," she added, seeing the sealed envelope on Susan's pile of presents.

"It's mine for Sally," Susan explained.

"Sally's Mum and Dad are giving her new clothes," said Jane. "What have you had?"

By the time Susan had described her presents, they had reached the school playground.

"Everyone's playing rounders!" Jane exclaimed. "Let's join in."

But Susan shook her head. A game of rounders might spoil her new clothes, and besides, she wanted to get her presents safely into the classroom. She went in through the big front door, down the passage past the Head's office and the staffroom, and through the hall to the cloakroom and classroom.

Almost immediately the bell for morning school clanged. Susan, her arms full of books, ran to the classroom bookcase, and took out the largest encyclopedia. How many pages had it got? Before she had discovered, the other children began pouring into the room.

"Happy birthday, Susan!" called Paula. "Oh!— you're wearing the same clothes as Sally."

"What?" Susan nearly dropped the encyclopedia.

"She's got a new pinafore and blouse just like yours. Where is she? We were playing rounders. Oh, there she is! Sally, come and look at Susan."

The throng of children parted, revealing Sally just inside the doorway. Susan stared at her aghast. After half an hour's rounders Sally looked hot and tousled. The collar of her blouse stood on end, and there was a muddy smear on her pinafore where she had fallen down. Susan felt as if she had been dragged in front of a distorting mirror. Sally looked so ridiculously like her; and yet like a rough, untidy Susan who had never existed.

"Where did you get those clothes?" she demanded.

Sally was more taken aback by Susan's manner than by the identical outfit. She had never bothered much about her clothes. "I don't know—I can't

45

remember the name of the shop," she stammered.

"Don't they look like twins!" someone exclaimed.

"They are twins; birthday twins."

And suddenly singing burst out.

> *"Happy birthday to you!*
> *Happy birthday to you!*
> *Happy birthday, dear twins!*
> *Happy birthday to you!"*

"Now nine tugs, and one for good luck."

Hands were thrust forward to pull the hair of the accidental twins.

Blazing with fury, Susan tore herself away. The presents and cards and encyclopedias tumbled to the floor.

"We aren't twins!" she shouted. "Sally just went and got herself born on my birthday."

"It's the same thing."

"It isn't!"

Alarmed by Susan's outburst, Sally tried to make peace. She pulled a crumpled envelope from her pinafore pocket.

"Here's a card for you, Susan," she ventured.

Susan snatched it contemptuously, too cross even to open it.

"Susan's got one for you, Sally," Jane told her. "Where is it, Susan?"

For a moment Susan didn't answer. She gave a little shrug to show that she had more important things than Jane's question to attend to, and bent to collect her scattered possessions. She pushed the school encyclopedia back into the shelf, picked up her books and writing case—and realized that her card for Sally had vanished. Susan didn't care.

"I haven't got a card for Sally," she said freezingly; and she stalked to her place, turning her back on her accidental twin.

Chapter Eight

IT WAS one of those school days when everything goes wrong. Books disappeared, pencils broke, and sellotape wound itself stickily round the fingers of the teacher, Mrs Wilson. And all the time, two undercurrents of gossip buzzed round the classroom. One, excited, ran—"Sally—barbecue—hot dogs—rounders—hide and seek." The other, shocked, ran—"Susan—bad temper—not Sally's fault—only accidental—accidental twins." Sally and Susan felt equally uncomfortable. They tried not to look at each other, and at dinner-time they kept as far apart as possible.

The day's final disaster came at the end of the afternoon. Someone in a hurry dislodged a shelf of the cupboard where the art materials lived, and paints, glue, and a mass of other things cascaded down in a sticky, multi-coloured flood.

"Well, really!" exclaimed Mrs Wilson. "Who's going to clear all that up?"

The child responsible for the disaster stared anxiously at his shoes. He was going to Sally's barbecue.

"Someone will have to help me," snapped Mrs Wilson.

Susan put her hand up. "I will," she volunteered.

"That's very kind of you," said Mrs Wilson, "but aren't you going to the ballet?"

"Not till Saturday," Susan answered.

"In that case, thank you very much. I know I couldn't have a better helper. I'll ring your mother from Miss Macdonald's office, and tell her you'll be late."

Mrs Wilson's praise soothed Susan's injured feelings. She had heard the mutterings against her, though she had pretended not to; and helping the teacher seemed a good way both of restoring her importance in the class, and of avoiding those moments in the cloakroom she had been dreading, when nearly everyone else would be going off to Sally's barbecue.

But Sally heard with astonishment that Susan wasn't going to the ballet till Saturday. She had been certain that Susan's birthday treat would take place on her birthday. Now she began to wonder if Susan's crossness that morning came from disappointment at not being asked to the barbecue, when so many others in the class were going. Was it too late to invite her? Sally knew her mother wouldn't mind. She had bought plenty of food for the expected crowd of hungry children. One more guest would make no difference.

The bell clanged. There was a rush for the door.

For a moment Sally hung back, uncertain. Susan saw her out of the corner of her eye. She walked stiffly to the cupboard, and began picking up paint palettes. Every inch of her back looked stubborn and unfriendly. Sally turned reluctantly away.

Mrs Wilson made Susan cover her new clothes with a large apron, and they set to work on their task. It was the sort of job that Susan liked. She worked hard till every shelf in the cupboard was spick and span, and she herself was happier than she had been since breakfast.

"Well done," said Mrs Wilson, as they washed their hands together. "I could do with a few more Susans in the class."

Susan smiled with pleasure. "I enjoyed it," she said.

"All the same, it was a funny birthday treat," observed Mrs Wilson. "Now I've got to lock up the Head's office and the staffroom, and then I'll lock the front door. See you in the playground. Right?"

"Right," said Susan.

She collected her coat, and then went back to the classroom for her presents and cards. At the back of her desk was the unopened card from Sally. Susan felt ashamed when she saw it. She needn't have been so unkind. After all, it had been an accident about the clothes, just as it had been an accident about the bouquet.

She ripped open the envelope, and pulled out the

card. A ballerina in a white tutu floated across the front of it. Susan stared at it guiltily. Like everyone else in the class, she knew of Sally's disappointment when her mother was unable to get ballet tickets, but in spite of that Sally had chosen her a ballet card, and Susan hadn't even said thank you for it. She felt horribly mean. And what had happened to her own card for Sally? Bundling her things together, crossing the hall, Susan tried to remember.

Mrs Wilson had locked the Head's office, and was going into the staffroom to fetch her coat.

"Ready to go, Susan?" she asked. "By the way, I must look at your new books some time. That's a lovely encyclopedia."

"It's got more pages than the one in our classroom—Oh!"

But Mrs Wilson had disappeared into the staffroom, and didn't hear Susan's half-stifled shriek.

Susan stood motionless. The encyclopedia in the classroom—Vividly, with absolute certainty, she remembered tucking the envelope for Sally inside the cover while she checked the number of pages.

Forgetting everything else, Susan dashed back to the classroom. She pulled out the encyclopedia and shook it. Out fluttered a sealed white envelope, with Susan's own writing on it—"To Sally Gray".

Thankfulness flooded over Susan. She suddenly knew that more than anything in the world she wanted to make friends with Sally, and here was the means of doing it. She would take the card straight to Sally's house, explain, apologize—and perhaps she would be asked to stay for the barbecue.

Gathering up her things again, she headed for the front door. She had just reached the passage, when the door banged shut. A key scraped in the lock, and Mrs Wilson's footsteps walked briskly away on the far side.

But she had said—"See you in the playground". Clearly she had thought that Susan was just going out when they had spoken about the encyclopedias, but as soon as she found the playground empty, she would come back. Of course she would.

Susan waited. Nothing happened. Far away, a car

engine revved, and purred out of earshot down the road. Susan's heart thumped. Mrs Wilson couldn't just abandon her like that—she couldn't.

It was dark in the passage, silent and eerie. Tall cupboards loomed like monsters in the shadows, and panic broke over Susan in a cold, shivering wave. She flew to the locked door, and pressed her mouth against the crack.

"Mrs Wilson!" she shouted. "I'm still here. Mrs Wilson!"

But nobody answered, and nobody came.

Chapter Nine

THE BARBECUE guests were enjoying themselves in Sally's garden. Tony had tried to start an immediate game of rounders, but it hadn't been popular. Rounders seemed ordinary compared with the tree house and the tyre swing.

"Which are the best trees to climb?" called Jane, and Sally pointed out her favourites.

But all the time a strange unease nagged in a corner of her mind. "What about Susan?"

"I'm staying here!" shouted Jane from the top of the beech tree. Sally ran to the yard behind the house, where her mother had set up the barbecue with its glowing charcoal stove.

"Mum," she burst out, "I wish I'd asked Susan."

"Give her a ring now, and suggest she comes down," said Mrs Gray.

"She isn't at home," Sally explained. "She stayed behind at school to help Mrs Wilson. Could I go and fetch her?"

"All right," said her mother. "You'd better go now."

Sally sped down the road, but as she reached the

gate at the top of the playground, a stab of uncer-
tainty stopped her in her tracks. She remembered the
aloofness of Susan's back when she picked up the
paint palettes, and the look on her face as she stared
unbelievingly at Sally's new clothes. Would Susan be
glad of the invitation, or would she be cold and snubbing?

I've got to ask her now, Sally thought. I told Mum
I would. But that wasn't the only reason. Quite
simply, she didn't like not being friends with
Susan. They were twins, and it was their birthday,
when everything should be pleasant. All the same, it
was quite likely that Susan would not feel as she did,
and Sally realized she didn't want a snub in front of a
teacher. Mrs Wilson's car was parked outside the
lower playground gate, so the cleaning up wasn't finished. Sally decided to wait until Susan came out.

She sat on the wall, swinging her legs, the sun
warm on her back. Presently she heard the bang of
the school door, and looked up. Mrs Wilson, hurry-
ing to her car outside the other gate, waved cheer-
fully. "Thanks again, Susan. Good-bye!" she called
and was gone.

Sally gazed after her in perplexity. What did Mrs
Wilson mean? She glanced round, but the playground was empty, and she was certain Susan hadn't
come out. What had happened?

And suddenly she understood. Mrs Wilson had
made the same mistake as the secretary had made.

She had confused one accidental twin with the other. Thinking Susan was safely outside in the playground, she had locked the school door, imprisoning poor Susan inside. And on her birthday too!

Sally looked up and down the road, but there was no one whose help she could ask. She knew that the caretaker lived in one of a nearby row of houses, but they all looked alike, and she didn't want to go knocking at every door until she found him. It would be better and quicker to rescue Susan all by herself.

Anyone less intrepid than Sally might have been at a loss, but Sally knew very well that doors do not provide the only entrance to a building. She and her brothers had climbed through windows since they were tiny. With experienced eyes she surveyed the school, wondering which window to try. Once in, she was sure she could persuade Susan to scramble out.

It was an old-fashioned school, built in the days when children were expected to keep their eyes on their books, undistracted by the sight of the world outside. The window-sills were all well above Sally's head, but that didn't deter her. She scanned the nearest wall carefully, searching for footholds.

Outside the hall a convenient drainpipe coincided with a crack in the stonework where some mortar had crumbled away. Sally put her left foot on the drainpipe and her right toe in the crack, stretched upwards, and pulled. A moment later she was standing on the outside window-sill, peering down into the hall below.

From high up the hall seemed mysteriously different. The cupboard tops were dusty and unpainted, while the polish on the floor had been worn away in tracks which crossed and recrossed between the doors. She was staring, fascinated, when the door from the front passage burst open, and Susan rushed through, tear-stained and frantic.

"Susan!" shrieked Sally, banging on the glass. "Susan!"

The change on Susan's face, as despair turned to joy, was like sunshine breaking through black clouds. She had run back, terror-stricken, from the dark passage to the hall, certain that she was trapped in school for the night. Now rescue was at hand—rescue in the unexpected shape of her accidental twin.

"Open the window!" called Sally.

Susan studied the window, her hopes sinking. It didn't open properly. Like all the windows it simply had a ventilator at the top, operated by a long cord.

"It's no good," she shouted despairingly.

"Pull!" Sally shouted back.

Something in her voice made Susan obey. She tugged the cord, and the ventilator tilted, leaving a narrow gap, hardly enough for a cat to squeeze through.

But it was enough for Sally. She jumped, heaved,

and squirmed through the crack, dropped on to the window-sill inside, and leaped down on to the floor. Her pinafore and blouse were even more rumpled and filthy, but Susan didn't care.

"Oh, Sally!" she cried. "I *am* glad to see you! I thought nobody would know where I was, and I'd be stuck here for the night. It was awful! I thought of ringing home, only Mrs Wilson had locked the office, and then I didn't know what to do. I'm so glad you came!"

"I came to ask you to my barbecue," said Sally; and they both burst out laughing, because it seemed so silly that Sally should have had to climb through the window to give her invitation.

"I would like to come—if only we can get out," said Susan. "I don't know why Mrs Wilson locked me in."

"She mistook me for you." And Sally explained what had happened. "Now," she finished, "if we're going to my barbecue we'll have to climb out through the ventilator."

Susan looked horrified. "I couldn't—not possibly! It's far too high. I might fall, or break the glass and cut myself."

"You wouldn't. It's easy. Watch me."

Sally pushed a chair under the window-sill, but before she could get on to it, Susan clutched her arm.

"I shan't be able to do it, and you mustn't go and leave me. I couldn't bear to be left on my own again."

"Just while I get help—"

"No!" cried Susan, shaking with fright. "No! You must stay with me."

"All right; I'll stay. Someone's sure to realize in the end where we are."

"Thank you," said Susan, very humbly. "You are kind. I'm sorry I was so horrid this morning. Look, here's my card for you. I found it after all."

Sally opened it, and looked delighted. "It's the prettiest one I've had. You must look at all my others when we get home. Oh dear, how long do you think we'll be stuck? I'm hungry."

"So am I," agreed Susan.

"Mum'll be cooking the hot dogs. We must get out."

"How?"

They stared helplessly round the hall; at the high impassable windows, the useless doors, the cupboards, the shelf with the school bell—

"The bell!" exclaimed Susan.

"We can ring it!" shouted Sally.

They rushed for the shelf, and Sally reached it first. She pulled the bell down, and shook it with all her might. The din echoed round the hall, and out through the doors and windows.

"Let me!" Susan seized it, and clanged it in her turn. One after another they rang the bell, loudly, hopefully, continuously.

The door flew open. The caretaker's wife bustled in, her expression a mixture of alarm and astonishment.

"Goodness, gracious me. You naughty little things! Whatever are you up to? I thought the school must be on fire."

Susan and Sally nearly fell over each other in their eagerness to tell the story.

"Well, I never!" said the caretaker's wife. "What a shame! No one's ever been locked in here before. And what are your names, my dears? I can see you're twins."

Those fatal words. Sally glanced nervously at

Susan, but Susan only laughed.

"Yes," she said, "we are twins, and it's our birthday today. I'm going to Sally's barbecue, and on Saturday she's coming to the ballet with me."

"Am I?" gasped Sally.

"Of course you are. There's a spare ticket, and Mum won't have rung Aunty Enid yet. Shall we wear our pinafores at the theatre, so that everyone can see we're twins?"

"I didn't know there were twins in the school," said the caretaker's wife.

"Oh yes, there are," said Susan. "At least," she added, "there are accidental twins."